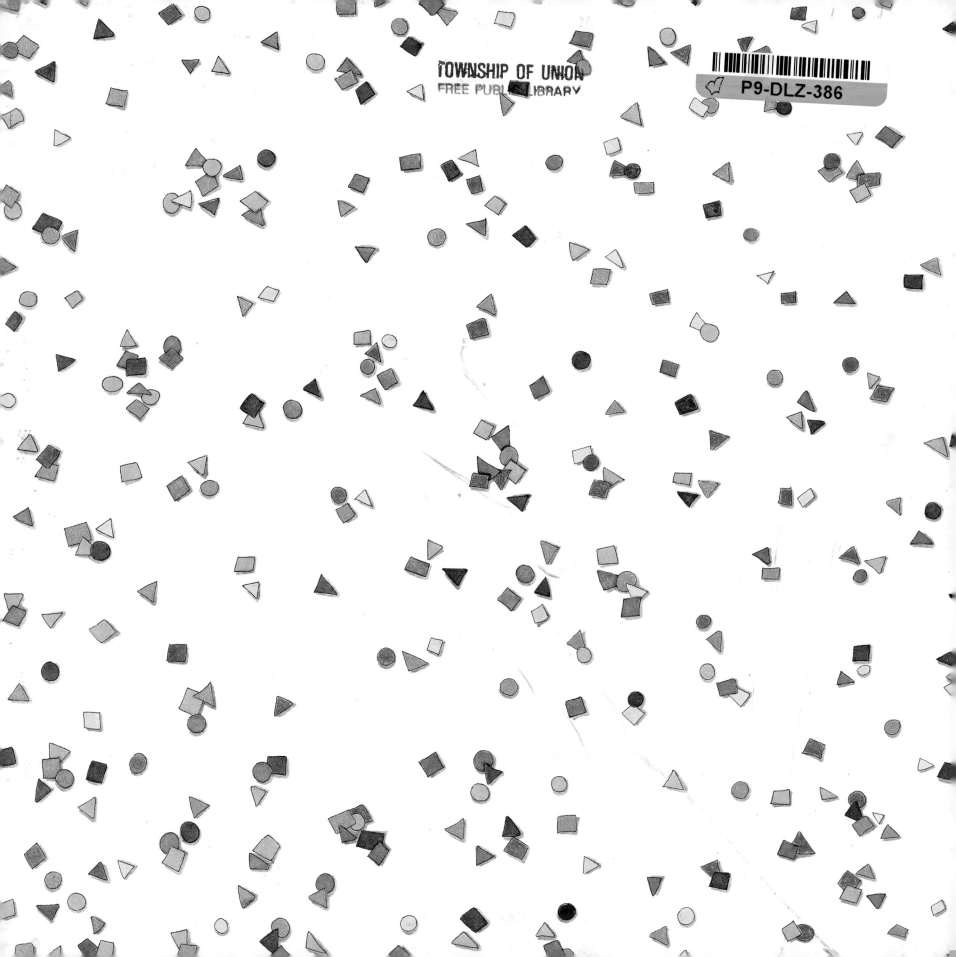

Little Albert's Birthday

For all the May babies
I know and love:
Sandra, Faye, Jessica,
Murray, Scott, Patrick,
Sidney, Carole, J,
Georgie & Gracie,
and of course, Albert

—L.T.

Albert's
Young-Adult
Birthday

Albert's
All-Grown-Up
Birthday

When Patsy plans a party, it's perfect. So, when she decided to give her best friend Albert a surprise party for his all-grown-up birthday, everyone knew it would be a perfect party.

Once Patsy had the party planned, she called a secret meeting of Albert's friends. On her special pad she had written out a task for each of them, described in detail. "I've chosen a spring theme," she said. "Flowers, flowers, flowers. It will be a flower extravaganza!"

The party would be in the school multipurpose room at 4:00 on Friday afternoon.

"But how will you get Albert to his surprise party if it's supposed to be a secret?" Sir Cedric asked.

ALBERT'S BIRTHDAY

SPECIAL THANKS TO TWO FRIENDS EXTRAORDINAIRE:

SHELLY KLINGENSMITH LYON, FIRST-GRADE TEACHER,

and CON PEDERSON

Albert's Birthday

WRITTEN

AND

ILLUSTRATED

by

LESLIE

TRYON

ATHENEUM BOOKS *for* YOUNG READERS

Albert's Birth Day

Baby Albert's Birthday

Albert's Teen Birthday

Atheneum Books for Young Readers   An imprint of Simon & Schuster Children's Publishing Division   1230 Avenue of the Americas New York, New York 10020   Text and illustrations copyright © 1999 by Leslie Tryon   All rights reserved, including the right of reproduction in whole or in part in any form.   Book design by Michael Nelson   The text of this book is set in Cooper.   The illustrations are rendered in pen-and-ink with watercolor.   Printed in Hong Kong   10   9   8   7   6   5   4   3   2   1   Library of Congress Cataloging-in-Publication Data: Tryon, Leslie. Albert's Birthday / written and illustrated by Leslie Tryon.—1st ed.   p.   cm.   Summary: Patsy Pig plans a surprise party for her friend Albert, giving careful instructions to all their friends, but she forgets to invite the guest of honor. ISBN 0-689-82296-0   [1. Birthdays—Fiction. 2. Parties—Fiction. 3. Animals—Fiction.] I. Title. PZ7.T7865Alh 1999 [E]—dc21   98-36621

7/02
$16.00

IP
TRY
c.1

FIRST EDITION

Patsy held up a note and read it out loud:

Memo:

From: Patsy Pig, PTA

To: Georgie and Gracie
Bess
Sir Cedric
Albert
Ms. Klingensmith, faculty advisor
Mrs. Golden

Subject: Committee meeting

* * * * * * * *

There will be an important committee meeting Friday, 4 pm, in the school multipurpose room.

"THIS is his 'invitation'!" Patsy said. "We know that Albert NEVER misses a committee meeting."

Patsy pushed the memo deep into her pocket. "All right," she said, "it's Tuesday. Bring your projects to the multipurpose room by 3:30 on Friday."

Everyone agreed that this truly was a perfect plan.

Patsy's Party Planner

🌸🌸

To: Ms. Klingensmith and her first graders

Your Task: Party hats! Tons of them. Paper hats with flowers, anything that goes with the garden theme. For example:

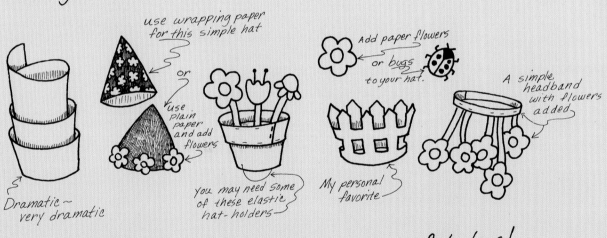

use wrapping paper for this simple hat

or

use plain paper and add flowers

Dramatic~ very dramatic

You may need some of these elastic hat-holders

Add paper flowers or bugs to your hat.

My personal favorite

A simple headband with flowers added

Thank you <u>so</u> much. You're fabulous!

Patsy

On Wednesday, the first graders began work on the party hats.

Patsy's Party Planner

To: Georgie, Gracie and Bess

Your Task: Your sensational apple treats. I recommend caramel apples, cinnamon applesauce and dried apples. You could bring the treats to the party in those marvelous antique wagons you have. What a lovely presentation.

Thank you so much, you're very dear,

Patsy

P.S. I'll send along some antique dresses for you to wear.

And on Wednesday, Georgie and Gracie made apple treats, and Bess got right to work on the wagons.

Patsy's Party Planner

To: Mrs. Golden

Your Task: A HUGE birthday card that carries out our flower theme. Please make this card large enough for everyone to sign. Perhaps it could look like this.

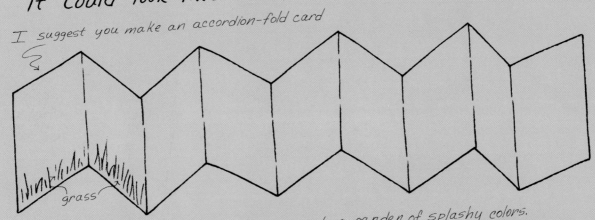

I suggest you make an accordion-fold card

grass

If you use tempera paints you can create a garden of splashy colors.

Albert will treasure it forever. Patsy

On Thursday, the puppies folded and painted a huge card.

And on Thursday, Sir Cedric began work on the cake.

Finally it was 3:30 on Friday, and everything was ready.

There were three ladybug flowerpots made by Patsy,

party hats with bouncing bugs and blossoms,

and a fleet of wagons to carry sweet apple treats.

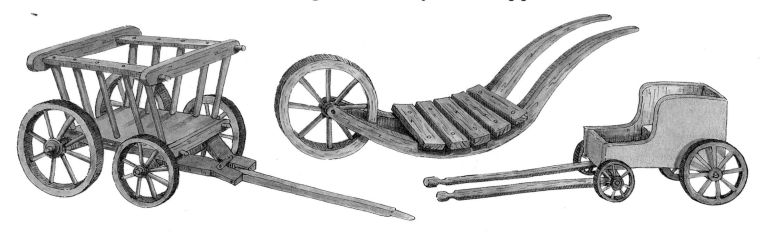

They all signed the huge birthday card.

At exactly 3:59 pm, Sir Cedric lit the candles on the flowering birthday cake and Patsy turned down the lights. "Shhh!" she whispered. Everyone got quiet as they waited for Albert to arrive. But . . .

. . . something was terribly wrong.

Patsy felt a piece of paper in the bottom of her pocket. It was the note! "I've made a terrible mistake," she said. "I forgot to deliver the note to Albert!"

This was a big problem, but as usual, Patsy had a solution. "If Albert can't come to his party," she said, "then we must take the party to Albert." As she marched out the door, she shouted, "To Albert's house!"

By the time Patsy and the party parade marched onto
the playground near Albert's unusual house, Albert had
locked his door and left. Where was he going?

"Albert? He just left," Frog said. "He is on his way to the bakery to get some chocolate cupcakes."

The paraders had been excited about taking the party to Albert's house, but now what would they do?

"Quick, my friends," Patsy shouted, "to the bakery!"

HAPPY BIRTHDAY

"You just missed him," Sir Cedric's assistant said. "He went to the apple farm to get a sapling for his garden."

"Come now, let's not dawdle," Patsy said. "Off we go to the apple farm!"

And so the party parade followed Patsy
out Long Valley Road to the apple farm.
It was a long walk and they were pooped!
Still, they hoped they weren't too late.

Saplings
Young apple trees
for your garden

Oh no! Just seconds after Patsy and the party parade entered the barn to look for Albert, he came out of the orchard. They had just missed him.

Albert was about to head home when he heard someone call his name . . .

"Hey! Albert, wait!"

When Albert followed Benny into the barn, he saw
a discouraged and tired group of friends. The rooster
crowed, and Albert shouted, "Surprise!"

Boy, were they ever surprised! Sir Cedric quickly lit
the candles on the flowerpot cake, and they all sang
"Happy Birthday" to Albert.

"A surprise party at the apple farm!" Albert said.
"What a brilliant idea. I never suspected a thing."

"It was Patsy's idea," Sir Cedric said. "Patsy is
the best party planner in the whole wide world."
And everyone agreed. It was just about perfect.

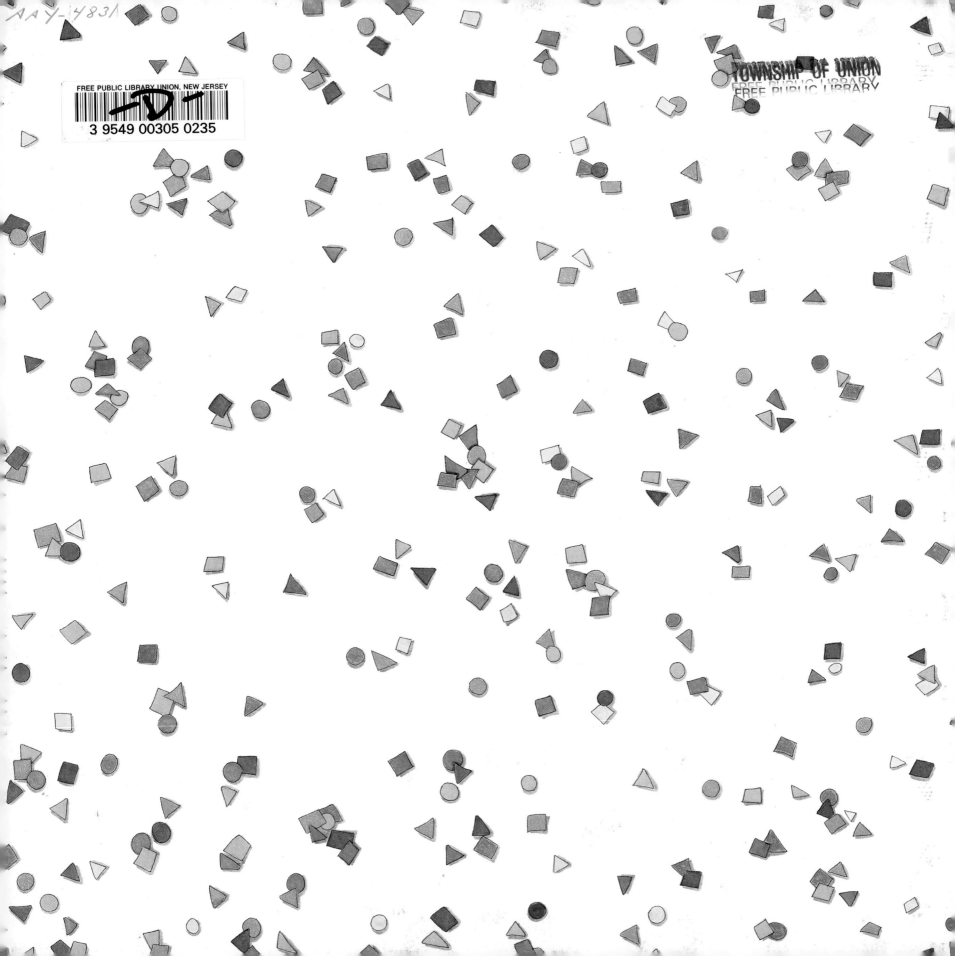